A **SporTellers**™ Book

HIGH ESCAPE

EVE COWEN

 CHILDRENS PRESS, CHICAGO

SporTellers™

Catch the Sun
Fear on Ice
Foul Play
High Escape
Play-Off
Race to Win
Strike Two
Stroke of Luck

Childrens Press Edition

Senior development editor: Christopher Ransom Miller

Content editor: Carol B. Whiteley

Production editor: Mary McClellan

Design manager: Eleanor Mennick

Illustrator: Bob Haydock

Cover: Bob Haydock

ISBN 0-516-02264-4
Library of Congress Catalog Card Number: 80–82986
Printed in the United States of America.
1.9 8 7 6 5 4 3 2 1

Contents

CHAPTER

Winter Games 1

"Switzerland!"

Dory Lane shouted the word as she turned to press her nose against the train window and watch the snow-covered land roll by. She couldn't believe that she was really there—in Switzerland, with its steep mountains, storybook houses, and deep blue lakes. Dory had always dreamed of going there one day. And now her dream had come true.

"You'll go right through that window in a minute," the man next to her said.

Dory turned to grin at the man who had spoken. It was Steve Mathews, Dory's skiing coach.

"I know that big grin is for Switzerland," said Steve. "But keep it for Irina Kapov too.

1

Let her think you don't have a care in the world."

"I don't have any cares," said Dory. "I'm going to take that gold medal. I just know it."

A woman who sat behind Dory moved forward in her seat. "I'm glad to hear you say that," the woman said. She was a teammate of Dory's, and her name was Barbara Cole. "I sure hope you're right," Barbara went on. "You've got the best chance of anyone on our team to do it. Wouldn't it be something if we beat Kapov—and the rest of the Russian team too?"

Dory nodded. She and all the other members of the U.S. Alpine Ski Team dreamed of beating the Russians in the International Alpine Ski Races in Mürren. They were on the way there now, winding slowly up the train track that would take them to the tiny mountain town. The train was the only way to get there—from Geneva to Lauterbrunnen, then up the steep mountain to Mürren. Dory sat back in her seat as she started to think about what lay ahead.

It was the first time Dory would be skiing in the International Alpine Ski Races. But she had spent most of her life on skis. And she had skied against Irina Kapov in the giant slalom several times before, once in Dory's home state of Colorado. Dory had lost to her every time. But this time she felt sure she would win.

Dory thought about the Russian skiing star. She remembered Irina's short yellow hair and her strong face. And she remembered that Irina had won the gold medal in giant slalom skiing for four years running. She had won an Olympic gold medal too. It seemed as if Irina Kapov could do no wrong on skis. The Russian had grace and style, and she never made a bad move.

Dory remembered that when she was 15, she had sent Irina Kapov a letter. She had liked Irina's style more than any other skier's in the world. And she had told her so. Irina had answered her with a letter that said how happy Irina had been to hear from an American friend. The letter had not said much more. But Dory had kept it for a long time.

The first time they met, Dory told Irina about the letter. But Irina did not remember it. "I hear from so many people," Irina had said. "So many people write letters to me."

Well, Dory thought with a grin. Things are different now. Kids from all over the world are writing to *me*. And even though Irina didn't remember me before, I'll bet she remembers me now.

* * *

The train pulled into the quiet Mürren station soon after the sun had gone down. As the members of the ski team piled out, a light snow began to fall. The team started walking toward the center of town, pointing out steep-roofed houses and beautiful storefronts. The whole place had a dreamlike air about it.

Soon the stately old Palace Sporthotel came into sight. The U.S. skiers would be staying there. So would the Russians.

After putting away their clothes, Dory and the other skiers headed for the hotel restaurant. Irina Kapov was there, having dinner with her teammates. Dory and Irina waved at one another across the room. Dory smiled. Irina didn't.

"I wonder what's the matter with her," Dory whispered to Barbara.

"She probably doesn't want to get too friendly with the person who's going to beat her," Barbara said. "Now let's forget about skiing and think about the great dinner we're about to order."

After dinner everyone but Dory decided to go out to see the rest of the town. "Not me," said Dory. "I'll do that kind of thing after the races are over. Right now I'm going back to my room to get some sleep. I want to be fit to check out the course inch by inch tomorrow."

"OK," Steve said. "But don't push too hard. You should have a little fun too."

"I'll have fun—racing," Dory said. "See you on the slopes first thing in the morning."

Steve smiled as Dory left the crowded restaurant. He knew that Dory had only one thing on her mind. She wanted to win the gold medal. And he understood what that felt like. Steve had been an Olympic skier before he became a coach. Skiing had been his life. And now, as coach, it still was. But he had learned that skiers skied better if they could take their minds off the slopes every now and then.

"OK," he called after Dory. "I'll be there. But later we're going to take some time off."

* * *

The sun had been up for only an hour when Dory got to the ski lift. The air was clear and cold, and the sky was blue. The steep white mountains that rose almost straight up around Mürren seemed very close. Dory thought it was one of the most beautiful sights she had ever seen.

As she pulled on her brown and orange hat, she looked around her. Steve Mathews wasn't there. Too early for him, Dory thought. The ski lift wasn't even running yet, but Dory wouldn't have used it anyway. She wanted to check over the giant slalom course carefully, and the only way to do that was on foot. Dory decided to look for Steve again after her first run. She shouldered her skis and started the long climb up the slope. The fresh snow looked soft and welcoming.

Dory knew that winning the giant slalom could depend on how well she knew the course. She would have to be fast—racers sometimes reach a speed of 40 miles per hour on the straight downhill run to the finish line. And the skier with the fastest total time would win. She would have three runs down the hill to come up with the best time. But it was not as easy as it sounded. She would have to zigzag down the hill between poles, called gates. To do that well, she had to learn the course by heart. She had to know where the snow was packed down hard and where it was soft. She had to know where there was ice below the new snow. She had to learn how much space there was between gates. She had to lock in her mind where every bump on the slope would be.

So Dory walked over every inch of the course. It took her a while. But by the time she reached the top, she had a good idea of what the race would be like. It would be tough. But she could do it. She would be in control.

Dory put her skis down and looked around. Everything was still. She felt as if she were alone at the top of the world. The ring of mountains around her looked wild, almost frightening. I wouldn't want to get lost out there, Dory found herself thinking. I have a feeling I would never find my way out.

"Is beautiful, yes?"

The voice she heard behind her made Dory jump. She turned. Irina Kapov was skiing toward her. Dark glasses covered her face.

"You surprised me," Dory said as she let out a big breath of air. "How did you get up here? Did you fly?"

"I come on ski lift," Irina said. Irina skied to an easy stop. She rested her glasses on the top of her ski hat.

Dory looked over at the lift. It was moving now, but there were no skiers on it.

"I walked up," Dory said. "I checked the course over. Now I'm ready to head down." She started to put on her skis.

"I have been in Mürren two days," Irina said. "I have gone down slope many times."

Still looking down, Dory thought, I wonder what she's trying to tell me? That she's way ahead? Her skis on, she stood up and faced

Irina. To her surprise, the Russian was staring at her with a strange look on her face. She didn't speak to Dory. She seemed to be thinking hard about something.

Dory waited a second, but still Irina didn't talk. Dory decided it was time to leave. "See you later," she said to Irina. Then she lifted her ski poles to push off.

"Wait," Irina said suddenly.

Dory turned and looked hard at Irina. The Russian seemed to want to speak but could not. Dory tried to help her. She asked, "Is something wrong?"

Irina reached out and put her hand on Dory's arm. "Please," she said. "We must talk."

"Talk? What about? The race?" Dory shook her head. "I really don't think we should."

"No, not race," said Irina. "Race means nothing to me." Then she turned suddenly and looked toward the ski lift. A couple of ski racers were now riding up on it. Soon they would be getting off at the top.

Dory couldn't believe her ears. "What do you mean, the race means nothing?"

Irina was still staring at the ski lift. The skiers who had been sitting on it had just reached the top of the run. In a few seconds they would be standing right next to Dory and Irina, ready to start their run down.

"Not now," said Irina as she watched the skiers move toward her. "There is no time now. We meet later." She put her glasses back in place.

"I'm not sure we should," said Dory.

"Tonight," Irina whispered. "After dinner. We meet. I think you will help me. Yes, I know you will." She stopped and looked hard at Dory. Then she went on. "Tell no one."

Without another word, the Russian star pushed off down the course.

Dory stared after her. What in the world is going on? What does she want me to help her with? This is really strange, she thought. Dory set her poles deep into the snow and said to herself, "I've got a run to make."

She pushed off down the slope, now marked with Irina's trail.

Looking Ahead 2

The cold air hit Dory's face like a sharp blow. It seemed to send the blood racing through her body. She moved out fast, bending low to pick up speed. All she could hear was the dry, cutting sound of skis on snow.

As she skied down the trail, she could see Irina ahead of her. The Russian moved with the grace of a bird, sailing down the hill. Dory followed fast. She felt as if she were already in the race with Irina.

Then, suddenly, the gates were in sight. Dory saw Irina zigzag through them. She finished without touching even one.

Then, just as suddenly, Dory was at the first gate. It came up too fast. She almost smashed into it. Just in time, she moved inside it and headed for the next one. Pushing hard with her poles, she cleared every gate without any more trouble and flashed down the open run to the finish line.

Breathing fast, Dory pulled up short. Snow flew in front of her. She looked around, but Irina Kapov was nowhere in sight. Instead, Steve Mathews was at the sidelines waving to her. She skied over to him.

"A good first run," Steve said, looking pleased. "I saw you as you came over the hill and moved through the first gate. Looks like that was the only one to give you trouble."

"It was," Dory told him. "I walked the course before I came down. I knew where that gate was, but it still came up too fast. I almost smashed into it," Dory said as she shook her head. "I'll have to work on that one."

"Again and again," said Steve. "Let's walk the course together now. Oh," he added, as they headed for the slope, "I saw Irina Kapov come down ahead of you. Did you two meet?"

"We sure did. I thought I was an early bird, but so is she," Dory said. "And on top of that, she said she already knows the course. She's been here for two whole days. She really has a head start."

"So you two talked a little bit," Steve said.

"Sure, why not? We've met before."

Steve went on. "What did you talk about? Anything besides who came to Mürren when?"

For some reason, Dory did not want to tell Steve about her strange talk with Irina Kapov. "Nothing really," Dory said. "Nothing of interest." She had reached the foot of the course and started to take off her skis.

"When two top skiers meet on a course and talk, it's got to be interesting," said Steve.

Dory stood up and rested her skis on her shoulder. "Something interesting like asking me to throw the race? Is that what you're thinking?"

"Why would I think that?" Steve waited a second and then asked another question. "Well, did she?"

"She didn't say anything," Dory told him. "I mean it. Now let's just forget it." As she looked at Steve, she thought, That's really just what happened. Irina talked to me. But really she had said nothing.

* * *

Dory and Steve went over the course together inch by inch. They worked on the best way to ski it. They checked every bump and hole, every spot of ice and bank of snow.

As they walked, they passed Irina and her coach checking the course too. Dory looked at Irina, trying to read her face. But Irina did not look at Dory. In fact, she acted as if Dory were not even there.

When Steve and Dory passed Irina a second time it really seemed strange that the Russian star still didn't look at or speak to Dory. Steve was surprised. "I thought you and Irina had talked before. Why doesn't she say hello?"

"Maybe she's afraid she'll be put in jail for speaking to an American," Dory said.

"Come on, Dory," Steve said. "Things aren't like that in Russia. Besides, it's skier against skier, not country against country."

"Dream on," said Dory. "You and I both know one thing. The Russians want their team to win. Then everyone will say what a great country Russia is. I've often wondered what happens to people like Irina if they don't win."

"Nothing happens to them," Steve said. "They win some, and they lose some. Just like American skiers. No one tells you to get lost if you lose a race. No one tells that to the Russian skiers if they lose."

Dory stared at Steve. "How can you really know?"

"Because Irina Kapov couldn't ski as well as she does if she were shaking with fear."

She may not be shaking with fear, Dory thought. But something's wrong. And I guess I'll find out what it is tonight.

* * *

"Penny for your thoughts," Barbara Cole said.

Dory turned her head. She had been watching Irina Kapov on the other side of the hotel restaurant. The Russian was having dinner with her teammates and coach. Two men in dark clothes were also sitting at Irina's table. They did not seem to take part in the talking. They just sat there looking stiff and angry.

"I'm sorry," Dory finally said to Barbara. "What did you say? I wasn't listening."

Barbara spoke again. "What are you staring at?"

"Oh, nothing," Dory said. "I guess I'm tired." She looked down at her food and wondered about Irina. The Russian's words came back to her: *I have to talk to you. After dinner.* Where after dinner? What was it all about?

"You'd better get with it," Barbara was saying to her. "You haven't heard one word I've said."

Dory tried to act interested in her friend. "Sorry," she said again. "How did your day go?" Barbara would be racing the downhill against the top racers from East Germany and France. Barbara might finish close to the top, but she did not think she would win a medal.

"My day went fine," Barbara said. "I push hard, but the others are too good."

Steve Mathews had been listening. "No more shop talk," he said. "Let's go for a walk." Then he looked at Dory. "I want you to come along. It will just be for a few minutes."

Dory shook her head. "I'd rather sleep than walk." As she spoke, she saw Irina leave her table and move toward the steps that led to the rooms. Dory stood up fast. "Go ahead without me," she told her friends. "I'll see you all in the morning." She headed toward the steps and followed Irina.

As she reached the steps, she saw a door close at the end of the hall. It was a side door to the street. Dory looked at it and then ran down the hall. She opened the door and went out.

It was beginning to snow. The street was empty of people, and all was still. As Dory looked around in the dark, she thought for a second that she had been wrong. Irina had probably gone up to her room, not outside. Then, suddenly, she heard Irina's voice.

"Over here," Irina called in a soft voice, from behind a tree.

When Dory came closer, Irina put her finger to her mouth. "Shhh," she whispered. "Follow me." Dory trailed her to the back of the hotel. This is mad, she found herself thinking. What am I doing here?

At last Irina stopped. She checked to make sure there was no one around. She came close to Dory. "I have decided I must trust you," she said at once.

Dory stared at her.

"Yes, I cannot do it alone," Irina went on. "You are my true friend. We write letters to each other. If I do not trust you, I can trust no one."

Letters, Dory thought. But that was long ago. She started to speak, but Irina stopped her.

"You will help me then," Irina said.

Dory opened her mouth. Her breath was white in the cold air. "Help you do what? What are you talking about?"

Irina stared at her. "You must help me escape. I wish to defect to America."

CHAPTER 3

No Way Out

Dory's eyes opened wide. "Defect? Here in Mürren? It's not possible."

"I do not wish to ski for Russia anymore," said Irina. "It must be possible."

"Look out there," Dory said, pointing toward the mountains. "We're in the middle of nowhere. There are no cars and no roads to drive on. You can only leave by train. And as a famous Russian skier, you won't be able to get on the train without everyone knowing your business. You can forget about skiing over the mountains too, if that's in your head. It would be rough. There's no way to leave here that would work."

"You will help me," Irina said, giving Dory a big smile. "We leave at once."

"You're not listening to me," Dory said. "It just can't be done."

"Is good for you to help me," said Irina, not listening again. "Americans will be glad. You will become famous too."

Dory shook her head. "I'm famous enough, thank you. Irina, if you really want to defect, wait until the races are over and your team takes the train to Lauterbrunnen. There will be more people there, and it will be easy to hide. You can slip onto a train to Geneva. The American Embassy will be very happy to help when you get there."

Irina shook her head. "I am watched. KGB. Someone must buy ticket for me. Help me." She reached out and took Dory's arm. "Come, we must go at once."

Dory thought of the two men who had sat at Irina's table. They must be with the KGB—the Russian secret police. But then she pulled away. "Slow down," she said. "Don't you understand what I've been saying? You have to do things more slowly. Wait for the right time and the right place. And besides, I have a race to run tomorrow. I can't help you defect. Lots of Americans are waiting for me to race in the giant slalom—and win."

Irina looked at her and began to laugh. "Slalom race? I would win slalom race, not you. But I don't wish to race for Russia."

"Well, I just can't help you," said Dory. "I'm here to race—and that is what I'm going to do." She put her hands in her pockets and started to walk away. "I'll see you on the slopes in the morning," she called.

"Just a minute," Irina said as she caught up with Dory. "OK. You race tomorrow. We both race. And I let you win gold medal," she said. "Then you go with me to Geneva."

As soon as she finished speaking, she walked on ahead fast, leaving Dory behind.

"Just a minute! Wait!" Dory shouted after Irina, but the Russian was already turning the corner of the hotel. When Dory reached the corner, Irina was gone.

Dory walked slowly to the hotel door. She pulled it open and walked around the rose-colored chairs and wood tables. What a news story this would be, she thought. Irina Kapov, the famous Russian skier, wants to defect to the United States. And she wants Dory Lane of the U.S. team to help her! I can't tell anyone about it, though. And I can't *do* anything about it either, Dory thought. Not until the races are over anyway. That gold medal is still the most important thing in the world to me.

Then Dory stopped walking. She remembered Irina's parting words: *I let you win gold medal.* Did she really mean it? Dory couldn't believe that Irina would throw the race.

* * *

Dory hit the finish line at top speed and skied to a stop. She had just run her first race of the day. In the giant slalom, skiers raced the course three times. Each race was important. The winner would be the skier with the lowest total time.

As Dory waited at the bottom of the slope, a voice came over the loudspeaker:

Dory Lane, United States. 66.69 seconds.

A big shout came up from the crowd as Dory skied over to the sidelines. "Not good, not bad," she said to Steve.

"It's the best time so far," Steve said. "You're doing OK. Irina hasn't raced yet, but I'm sure you're making her worry."

Skier after skier followed the long zigzag course to the bottom of the slope. There were some bad spills. And many gates were knocked over. But the race went on.

When Irina came down the slopes, Dory was there to watch her. Again Irina's words came back to her: *I let you win gold medal.* But from the look of her race down the course, Irina wasn't letting anyone win anything. She hit the finish line at top speed. The crowd let out a shout.

Irina Kapov, Soviet Union. 66.18 seconds.

Irina had finished with the best time so far.

Dory looked at Steve. Worry showed all over her face. "Take it easy," Steve told her. "There are two more races to go before this is all over. Don't worry. You'll make it."

* * *

Here goes, Dory said to herself. Race number two. She stood at the top of the run, poles down, arms forward. She took a deep breath and pushed off hard as the starting gate opened.

Then the trouble began. The course was worn down. Too many skis had gone over it. She could see bumps and tracks everywhere in the snow.

Sitting down a little to take the bumping from the tracks, she went into the first gate too low. Suddenly she was down, her skis falling away. Trees on the sidelines were hanging from the sky. Ice burned her mouth as she went sliding toward the snowbank. With a rain of white, she hit the bank and lay still. People came running.

Dory sat up and caught her breath. Nothing seemed broken. She reached out for a helping hand and stood up. Someone on the sideline handed her her skis and poles. She put them on and headed down the hill. She would finish the race, but not with a fast time.

When Irina's turn came, it looked as if there were no way the Russian would lose. She seemed to be in complete control, moving in and out the gates.

Then, suddenly, Irina went down. It happened between the last two gates. It was a bad spill, but after a short time Irina got up and made it to the finish line. Her time was very slow. Dory took a deep breath. She and the Russian were even for this race. But Irina was still ahead.

Racer after racer had trouble with the course. A crew came to even it out, but their work didn't help much. No one had a very fast time for the rest of the day.

"That should make you happy," Steve said, when he and Dory heard all the finishing times.

"I don't know," said Dory. "Irina's still ahead." As she spoke, Dory couldn't keep from wondering. Did Irina fall to even things up? Is she really trying to lose because she wants my help?

* * *

The note lay at Dory's place at the dinner table. It was there when she sat down.

Steve Mathews pointed to it. "That's been waiting for you," he said.

Dory stared hard at the folded slip of paper. She couldn't see any writing. But she knew it had to be from Irina.

"Love letter," said Barbara, grinning at Dory from across the table.

"That's what it is," said Dory. She grabbed the paper and pushed it into her pocket.

"Hey, wait a minute," said Steve. "It's pretty funny to get a note and not even check it out."

"I'll read it later," said Dory. She gave a little laugh to cover her feelings of worry. "I like to read my love letters when I'm by myself."

She picked up her glass to drink but put it right down again. "Look, I'll be right back," she said, getting up from the table.

"Go ahead, read your love letter," Barbara said. Everyone at the table laughed and then started talking again.

Dory went into the next room and pulled the letter from her pocket. It was from Irina all right. It was written in simple English, like the letter from long ago. But the words were very different this time.

Hello friend, Irina had written. *Tomorrow is special day for you. Is special for me too. Remember.*

Dory read the letter again. Its words told her that Irina's fall had been forced to even up the race.

Dory folded the letter and put it back into her pocket. Irina really was going to throw the race. Dory was not sure what to do. She would have to decide.

She looked up and found Steve at the door watching her. "Come on now, out with it," he said, coming toward her. "That's no love letter. What's going on? Why the worried look?"

"I don't know what you're talking about," Dory said.

"If you're in trouble, you'd better let me in on it."

"Maybe you're right," Dory said after a few seconds. "I didn't want anyone to know about this before. But now I think you should. You'd better read this."

Steve took the note from Dory and read it slowly. Then he handed it back to her.

"OK, explain it," he said. "It doesn't mean a thing to me."

When Dory finished telling Steve everything that had happened, Steve shook his head. "I don't like this one bit. But I don't want you to think about it at all. You're here to race. And that's all I want you to think about. Racing—and winning. Irina Kapov can do anything she wants. But stay away from her while she's doing it. Just stay away from her."

CHAPTER 4

Fair and Square

Irina looked good in the warm-up early the next morning. "It doesn't look like she's planning to throw the race," Steve said as he and Dory watched Irina shoot down the course.

"She has to fool her coach," said Dory. "And the KGB. After all, she can't let them know what her plans are."

"I'm still not sure about all this," said Steve. "But my guess is that Irina isn't trying to throw the race. She's trying to throw *you*."

"Listen," said Dory. "Get this through your head, Steve. I've decided that no matter what she's trying to do, I'm not going to worry. I'm going into this race with an easy mind—a mind set on winning. Irina can race her heart out or not. I came here to win."

* * *

The third—and last—round of the giant slalom began. Dory waited her turn with the other skiers at the top of the slope. Again, she would race ahead of Irina.

Time moved fast. Skier after skier rushed out of the starting gate and down the hill. Before Dory knew it, it was her turn to race. As she waited to start, the course flashed through her mind. A short time ago the crew had built up the worn spots. It would be a fast track.

Then the starting gate opened. Dory pushed on her poles and moved out fast. The gates seemed to swim up to her. She curved her body to move between them, first to the left, then to the right. She passed through gate after gate, in complete control. When the last gate was behind her, she moved forward to pick up more speed. Then the downhill run was over. She crossed the finish line and heard her name shouted by the crowd. Dory had broken the time for that course and had set a new record.

As she started to ski to the side, her friends crowded around her. Barbara shouted, "65.72 seconds! You did it. You did it!"

Dory looked over at Steve and smiled. He smiled back, but his smile told her it wasn't over yet. Irina still had to race.

The day went on as skiers followed each other down the steep giant slalom course. No one came near Dory's time. But the crowd wondered if that would change as Irina started her run.

The trouble happened right away. Irina came speeding toward the first gate. It was the same one that had given Dory trouble in the second race. As Irina went into it she fell, taking the pole with her. She turned over and over while her skis flew high into the air. For a while, it seemed that she might roll and slide all the way down the hill. People were screaming. Then some began to run toward her.

Dory felt her heart pounding. She started to run toward Irina too.

Steve grabbed her and pulled her back. "There's nothing you can do. I see a doctor heading for her. Let him take care of her. Look, she's moving. She can't be hurt too much."

"No?" Dory pointed to a spot of red on the snow where Irina lay. "Look at that. It's blood."

"She'll be all right," said Steve. "But if we go over there, we'll just get in the way."

Dory and Steve watched as several skiers started to move people away from Irina's side. After a minute, Steve turned to Dory and said, "You know what this means, don't you?"

Dory was watching the doctor bending over Irina. Half listening to Steve, she asked, "What?"

"The gold medal is yours."

Dory turned to him and stared. "Yes," she said in a very soft voice. "I suppose it is."

* * *

"I just spoke to the Russian coach," Steve told Dory later that day. "Irina's OK. She has a bad cut on her face—the pole hit her as she dragged it down the slope. And her ankle is sprained, but she can walk. She's not supposed to put too much weight on it, though."

"I'm glad it's not any worse," said Dory. She had been given the gold medal for the giant slalom a short while before. But she still felt a little funny about getting it. She had wanted to win it, but she had also wanted Irina to finish the race.

"Irina won't be going very far on that foot," said Steve. "So I guess that puts an end to her plans for defecting."

"If that's what her plans were," said Dory.

"Well, we're leaving Mürren day after tomorrow," Steve told her. "If she defects, we'll read about it in the papers."

As Dory and Steve talked, they picked up their skis and headed for a cable car not far from the giant slalom course. They and all the other skiers and coaches who had been a part of the International Alpine Ski Races were taking cable cars to the top of Mount Schilthorn. At that high point there was a restaurant called Piz Gloria. It was big and round and had glass windows that looked out on the Bernese Alps. All the skiers who had been in the races would have dinner together at Piz Gloria and then ski back down the mountain, carrying lighted torches.

Dory and Steve joined several others for the cable car trip to the mountain. It was growing dark fast. The last light of the sun showed the beautiful hotel and the tall, straight trees below. People in the hotel would see a special sight when the skiers came down carrying their torches.

Dory and Steve and the rest of the U.S. team were already eating at the long wood tables when Irina and her teammates came into Piz Gloria. With them were the Russian coach and the two men in dark clothes. Irina had a bandage on her face. She limped as if she were in pain.

"That's pretty brave of her," Dory said to Steve. "Even if she can't join everyone skiing down the mountain later."

"I think she wants the whole world to see she was really hurt," said Barbara. "She wants them to know how bad the fall was— and why she didn't win."

"Maybe," said Dory. Then, suddenly, her heart began to pound. Irina was heading for the U.S. team's table. The two men wearing dark clothes followed her.

When the Russian ski star reached the table, she looked hard at Dory and held out her hand. "I give you my good wishes," she said. "You ran great race."

Dory nodded. She didn't know what to say. She reached out her hand and shook Irina's. Then she tried to keep a look of surprise off her face when she felt a piece of paper touch her hand. Irina had passed her a note.

With a smile, Irina turned and went to sit at her own table. Dory looked to Steve. "Another note," she whispered. "I'm afraid to look at it."

"She can't force you to do anything you don't want to do," Steve told her.

Dory slowly opened the note. *Meet me at cable car at 8 P.M.* She felt her heart sink. So Irina was going to go through with it after all.

Barbara looked at Dory and opened her eyes wide. "Another love letter?"

Dory didn't even try to answer her. She handed the note to Steve.

He read it and folded it up. "I guess she wasn't playing games. OK," he said. "Do you want to make that meeting?"

Dory looked at him. Then she nodded her head up and down. "Yes," she said. "I do."

"Then make it," Steve went on. "But I'm going with you."

"Hey," said Barbara. "What's going on?"

"Later," said Dory. "I'll tell you later."

For the rest of the dinner, Dory didn't say much. But happy voices rang out all over the room. It was a beautiful night, and everyone was enjoying it. Soon the dinner was over, and groups of skiers stood outside the restaurant putting on their skis. But not Dory.

Barbara looked at her. "Aren't you going to put your skis on?"

"You better go ahead by yourself," Dory told Barbara. Barbara shook her head as she took one of the flashing torches that were being handed out.

Steve and Dory watched Barbara ski over to where the rest of her team waited. Then they turned to watch the line of people who were taking the cable car to see the skiers from below. "Do you see her?" Dory asked Steve.

"No sign of her," Steve said. "Let's head for the cable car."

They had just about reached it when Dory saw the two Russian men on the other side pushing their way into the crowd. "The KGB," she said. "Quick! Check the cable car. See if she's already in there."

CHAPTER 5

High Above the Alps

"There she is," Steve called to Dory, "in the cable car. Quick, let's get in."

The door on the car was beginning to close. Dory and Steve pushed toward it through the crowd. People called out angry words. But the sight of the KGB men closing in kept Steve and Dory moving forward.

Finally they made it to the car. But the door was just about shut. Steve grabbed the handle and tried to pull it open.

"No more," the conductor shouted. "The car is full. You will have to wait."

For a second Dory stopped. We're not going to make it, she thought. She banged on the door. "Just two more," she begged.

The conductor made a face. Then he smiled. "Dory Lane! The giant slalom winner. All right, get in."

In seconds, Steve and Dory were in the car with the door closed behind them. They pushed their way to Irina's side.

"My skis," Dory said suddenly. "I left them behind at the restaurant."

"Don't worry about skis," said Irina with a cool smile on her face. Then she whispered, "I buy you new skis when we get to America."

Just then the cable car jumped out onto the thin wires that would take it down to the town below. Dory looked out through the window and saw the two Russian men waving their arms at the cable car, trying to get the conductor to stop it. Dory couldn't help it. She waved back at them.

In a few minutes, the cable car was high over the Alps, on its way to Mürren. The moon was full, but a few clouds were coming into sight. Below, skiers were beginning to move down the slope. Their bright torches looked beautiful against the snow.

Then, all at once, it happened. The cable car came to a stop. For a second, the people inside seemed glad. They had a minute to look out the windows at the skiers. But when the cable car didn't start moving again, they began to worry. French, German, Swiss, and English could be heard in the car.

Then someone shouted in English. "There are too many people on board. We're in bad trouble." Some of the crowd turned to stare at Dory and Steve.

"Do not worry," the conductor called out. "We'll be moving again soon. Everything will be all right."

"That's got to be a 1500-foot drop," Dory whispered to Steve. He looked just as worried as she did.

Suddenly there was a strange cracking sound. The lights in the cable car went out. The car went sliding forward with a rush, throwing everyone to the floor or across the crowded space. Then the car stopped, just as suddenly. But the quick stop made it swing as it hung from the wire.

Dory got to her feet slowly, holding on to the corner of the window. She was not hurt, but people around her were. Everyone was calling out or crying. The conductor tried to keep everyone still. But it was not possible.

Dory tried to find Steve. But it was too dark in the car to see him. She called, "Steve?" Then she called, "Irina?" She heard Steve calling her name, but in the fall he had been pushed to the other side of the car.

Finally Steve made his way over to Dory. "You OK?"

"So far," said Dory. "How about you?"

Steve nodded.

Dory asked another question. "You think we'll get out of here in one piece?"

"Sure," said Steve, but he didn't sound as if he believed it. "I talked to Irina. She was thrown to the other side too. She's OK," he said. "But someone fell against her leg."

As Steve finished speaking, the strange cracking noise started up again. They all held their breath. Then the car began to move forward, but slowly this time. Yes. It was on its way.

Far below, the bright line of skiers trailed down the mountain. The skiers never would have guessed what had happened above them. Steve and Dory watched the skiers through the window.

"Irina said that when we get back to Mürren we'll have to act fast," Steve told Dory in a low voice. "She's sure the KGB men will take the next cable car down the mountain. That means as soon as our car goes back up, it will bring those guys down. We'll have to get out of Mürren before they get there."

Dory looked at him. "Then we'll have to ski to Lauterbrunnen."

"Ski?"

Dory nodded. "I read all the train times on our trip from Geneva. No train leaves Mürren until tomorrow morning."

Journey 6
from Mürren

By the time the cable car reached Mürren, Irina's ankle was much worse. She needed help to walk. Dory and Steve helped Irina to a spot where they could work out their plans.

"There's no way you can ski to Lauterbrunnen with your ankle in that shape," Dory said.

"My ski boot will hold it stiff," Irina told her. "It is short trip to Lauterbrunnen."

Dory shook her head. She did not think Irina could make it. The journey from Mürren to Lauterbrunnen would take them down a steep mountain. It would probably take only an hour, but it would not be an easy trip.

Dory shook her head again. It would be very hard. But it was the only way the Russian star could get away. And now was a good time to go. Everyone in the little town was busy. Some people were helping those who had been hurt on the cable car. Others were meeting or watching the skiers coming down the hill. Dory, Steve, and Irina could probably put on their ski masks and leave town without anyone thinking about it. They just had to act as if they knew where they were going—and what they were doing.

"OK," said Dory. "We'll go. But Steve and I will have to go back to our hotel for our other skis. And we'll all have to get shoes, money, and passports. We'll need them when we get to Lauterbrunnen."

"Right," said Steve. "And I'll leave a note for Barbara to explain what's going on. I'll tell her not to check us out of the hotel, since we'll be coming back. And I'll tell her to keep still about everything."

"Let's meet in 15 minutes in front of the hotel," Dory said. "But let's try not to look like we're in a hurry." Then she thought for a minute. "We need two other things," she said.

Steve and Irina looked at her.

"A map. We will need it to get to where we want to go," Dory said. Then she looked at

Steve. "And a rope. We have to dig up some rope somewhere. We'll have to tie ourselves to Irina. With that bad ankle, we can't let her out of our sight."

Irina made a face. "Rope? I don't need rope. I don't have to be tied like baby."

Steve shook his head. "Dory's right," he said. "We need a rope. Just look at the sky. It's changed since dinner. A lot of clouds now. The moon is just about covered, and it feels like snow. We will have to keep track of you if it snows hard."

"I'll look for a rope," Dory said. "They must have one put away somewhere in the hotel. A lot of people come here in the summer to climb the mountains."

"That's it, then," Steve said. He turned to Irina. "We'll meet you in front of the hotel in 15 minutes. Dory and I will both look for a rope."

The two Americans watched Irina limp away. "I don't know how she's going to do it," Dory said.

"She's brave," Steve said. "And she wants to get away from the Russians. She'll do it— with our help."

* * *

Soon after, the three skiers were on the trail to Lauterbrunnen. Dory was in the lead. Irina was in the center. Steve was last. There was 10 feet of rope between each of them. It would let Steve and Dory know if Irina fell.

The map had shown a trail that followed the train tracks to a small town called Grütschalp. There the trail turned down the steep mountain toward Lauterbrunnen.

The trail was easy to follow during the first few minutes. Clouds still covered the moon. But the trail was packed down hard enough to feel and see in the lights from the town below. And the train tracks were a dark line across the white snow.

"This should be easy," Dory called over her shoulder once they were out of Mürren. They would get to Lauterbrunnen before anyone knew they were gone.

Then the wind came up. Slowly at first. But when they were almost to Grütschalp, a hard wind started to blow. With it came more snow. The snow began to fall in thick, white sheets.

Dory stopped and waited for Steve and Irina to catch up. "This is no good," she said. "I can't see the trail." The wind was so loud she had to shout for them to hear. She took off her glasses because she couldn't see through them. They were covered with snow. But when she took them off, her eyes began to hurt.

"We must go on," Irina shouted back.

Dory nodded her head. There was nothing else they could do. Pulling at her hat, she turned and went on.

Just moving through the wind and snow was a fight. It was like trying to push a heavy door open. Then Dory felt a pull on the rope. Irina had gone down. After Steve and Dory helped her up, they all moved with special care. Dory skied more slowly, with no thought of picking up speed or making better time. She kept stopping to check Irina. The Russian would not say it, but Dory knew that her ankle really hurt. Two more times Irina went down, and still they could not find Grütschalp.

CHAPTER 7

The House in the Snow

How long had they been gone? An hour? Two hours? Dory had lost track of time. All she could think about was one thing—as long as she and her friends kept going down the never-ending mountain, they would have to reach the bottom sometime.

Unless they flew off the side of the mountain first. That could happen. They might be skiing over the train tracks that ran along the side of the mountain right now. If Dory went past the tracks, she would fall over the side and pull Irina and Steve with her. They could fall right into Lauterbrunnen!

Easy does it, Dory told herself. This snow is driving you mad. And now is not the time to go mad.

She shook her head and forced herself forward. As she skied, she kept her eyes down. She had to watch for any change in the ground they were crossing, for any sign of the tracks. That was how she almost missed the spot of light. But it caught her eye. She looked up. For a second, she could see nothing but the falling snow. But when she moved forward a bit, she saw it again. It was a light in a window. She was sure of it.

She waved at Irina and Steve to catch up.

"There's a house over there," she shouted. "I saw a light in a window."

Irina tried to look through the thick snow. "Where?"

Dory pointed toward the spot where the light had been. It was gone. "I'm sure I saw something," she told her friends. "It was a light."

"It's easy enough to find out," Steve called through the wind. "Let's ski over there."

Dory headed toward the spot where she thought the light had come from. Suddenly, a great dark shape rose up in front of her.

"A house! This must be Grütschalp," Dory said. "We've come to Grütschalp!"

"Maybe," said Steve, catching up. "But where are the other houses? Grütschalp is a small town, I know. But only one house?"

"One house or ten, who cares? We're here, and that's all that counts," Dory said to him.

Irina had listened to Steve and Dory talk. She shook her head. "No. We must go on to Lauterbrunnen," she told them.

"Not now," said Dory. "First we are going to knock on that door and get help."

"But they will find us if we don't keep going," Irina said. "We must go."

"They will find us if we don't stop here," said Dory. "They will find three dead bodies under a lot of snow." She and Steve slipped off the rope that tied them to Irina. They skied up to the door.

Steve knocked. No one answered. After a minute he knocked again. He was just about to force the door when it flew open.

An old man stood in a dark hall and stared out at them. He held a lighted candle.

"I'm so glad someone is here," Steve said. He looked at the man. "We're lost. Can you help us?"

The old man shook his head. He did not understand anything that Steve had said.

"We're lost," Steve said again. "Lost. Do you understand me? Do you speak English?"

Just then, there was the sound of an engine behind them. They turned to see a snowmobile. A tall, thin man climbed out of it and came running toward them.

As he reached the door, he smiled at Dory and Steve with thin lips. "Skiers on a night like this! You must be lost. Come. Come in. I'm sorry if Johann didn't help you. He doesn't speak English."

Dory turned to Irina, who stood away from the house. "Come on, he won't eat you," she called. Irina would not move, so Dory went over to her. "It's not possible to go on in this storm, and you know it. Let me help you get that rope off."

"Is not good," said Irina, shaking her head. But she let Dory take off the rope. Then the three skiers took off their skis and masks and followed the tall man into the house. In the hall, they took off their packs and pulled out their shoes from them. They put the shoes on and walked into a room where a welcome fire burned.

Irina sat down in a big brown chair and made a face. Dory saw it. "Does your ankle hurt much?" She was afraid it would hurt more now that the boot was off.

Irina gave her a brave smile. "Not much," she said, but Dory could tell she was in pain.

"I'm Baron Schiller," the tall man said as Dory and Steve moved close to the fire. "And you are. . . ?"

Steve gave Baron Schiller some made-up names and explained what the three of them were doing in the storm. None of it was true, but it sounded good.

"We're staying in Mürren," he said. "We were doing some night skiing and got lost in the storm."

The baron lit several candles as Steve spoke, and he put one on a table where Irina sat. The candles lit up a large and beautiful room with many pictures on the walls. They also showed the bandage on Irina's face.

The baron stared at Irina. "Your cut must be bad. Are you feeling all right?"

"I fell today," Irina said. "Is a small cut, that's all."

"And the limp," Dory said suddenly. "She fell on the trail a while ago."

"It's just not her day," Steve added.

Dory was afraid they were talking too much. The baron did not say anything for a moment. He stared at all three of them. Then he smiled. "Well, I hope you will be comfortable. The lights are out, though, as you can see. And the telephone doesn't work either."

Dory wanted to smile but held back. Since the telephone was out, he could not get in touch with the Russians. That was good news.

The baron went on. "But you must have planned for trouble," he said. "The rope. Shoes."

"We were headed for Grütschalp," Steve said. "We had thought that we might have dinner there."

That explains the shoes, Dory thought. But what about the rope?

"Oh, and the rope was in case someone fell," the baron said. "Good idea. You Alpine skiers know what you're doing. But you're way off your trail. You've gone right past Grütschalp."

Dory gave a small laugh. "We're still in Switzerland, I hope."

The baron laughed too. "The last time I looked. And I hope you like it here. Because you'll have to spend the night. It's too bad out there to go on."

Dory looked at Schiller. What had he been doing out in his snowmobile? Had he been looking for them? Had he heard about Irina? Did the Russians want her back bad enough to tell everyone to be looking for her?

"It is bad," Dory said finally. "But it may get worse. Perhaps we should go on. I mean, it could snow for a week."

Irina stood up. It was easy to see that her ankle was really hurting. "Is best we go," Irina said, trying to hide the pain.

But the baron shook his head. "No need to. I have the snowmobile. Tomorrow I'll take you all back to Mürren, safe and sound."

Back to Mürren—that was just what they did not want!

The baron smiled. Dory didn't like that smile one bit. It was as cold and as mean as the wind outside.

On the Run 8

Russian!

Dory stopped dead in her tracks as she walked down the hall of the baron's house. Why was the baron speaking Russian—at five in the morning?

Dory and Irina moved closer to the door where the voice was coming from. "What is he saying?" Dory whispered.

Irina put her ear to the door. "He talks to someone on a radio. He knows who I am! He asks for helicopter to come here!"

Steve came up behind them. "What's the matter?"

"We're in big trouble," said Dory. "The baron has a two-way radio. And he speaks Russian. He has asked for a helicopter to come. Do I need to say more?"

"Well, it won't change our plans. But we will have to move even faster."

They had not gone to sleep at all. Instead they had stayed dressed and waited for the snow to stop falling. While they waited, they had checked the baron's snowmobile. They were in luck. In his hurry, the baron had left the keys in the lock.

And so they had a plan. Dory and Irina would take the snowmobile. Steve would keep the baron busy while they got away. As soon as he could, Steve would follow on skis.

Dory and Irina would go straight to Lauterbrunnen and hope to meet Steve there. But whether they met him or not, they would grab the first train to Geneva. They could only hope the Russians would not be waiting at the train station.

"Let's get going," Dory whispered. She led the others out of the house and into a clear morning. The snow had stopped. Then Dory remembered. "My skis. I left them inside. Do you think I'll get them back? That's two pairs I've lost."

Steve nodded. "Irina's are inside too. We can worry about them later," he said. "Right now you better get moving."

Irina was already in the jump seat. Dory sat down in front and reached for the key. "Let's hope it catches," she said. "After all, it's pretty cold out."

She held her breath and turned the key. The engine came to life at once.

"We're off," she shouted. The snowmobile shot forward. "See you in Lauterbrunnen," she called back to Steve.

She turned right as she pulled out in front of the baron's house. They had looked at their maps during the night and decided that the house was just outside of Grütschalp. A right turn would take them along the side of the mountain and into Lauterbrunnen. The run wouldn't take long.

As Dory drove over the soft new snow, she looked back. Steve was walking toward the house. He was going to tell the baron that Dory and Irina were headed back to Mürren. He was going to say that they hadn't wanted to wake up the baron. Then he was going to talk with the baron until Dory and Irina were well on their way.

* * *

The way to Lauterbrunnen was steep but clear. There were trees on both sides of the

path along the snow-covered mountain. Dory
and Irina were making good time. But suddenly Irina tapped Dory's shoulder. She
shouted above the noise of the engine.
"Helicopter!"

Dory called back, "Where is it?"

But Irina didn't have time to answer. In a
few seconds the helicopter was right above
them. It came down low and seemed to sit only
a few feet from the tops of their heads. It
stayed right there as the snowmobile raced
forward. It was going to stay with them all the
way to Lauterbrunnen.

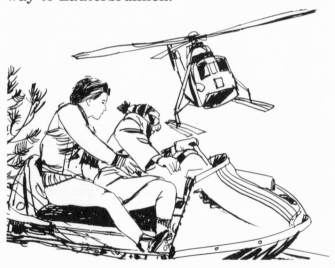

The noise of the helicopter roared in their ears. The force of the air it rained on them pushed the snowmobile from side to side. Dory thought that the big machine was like a giant bird that wanted to grab them and fly away. But it couldn't grab them.

Suddenly the trail shot the snowmobile into Lauterbrunnen. There were buildings on both sides of the street. The helicopter went up to miss the houses. Out of the corner of her eye, Dory could see it heading for an open field to set down in.

She headed for the train station. A train sat on the track. She would have to move fast to get there before it pulled out. And before the KGB landed the helicopter and got there themselves. The race would be close.

Dory turned onto a street that seemed to lead to the station. But it was a dead end. She had to turn around and go back. For a minute, she couldn't decide which street to turn on.

"Take next street," Irina ordered.

Dory turned the snowmobile into the next street. The station was straight ahead. She raced forward and then cut the engine. "Let's go, Irina," she shouted as she jumped out.

Then she saw some smoke shoot out of the train's engine. The train was ready to leave.

Irina stepped off the jump seat, but her ankle was in bad shape. She slipped and went down. "Help me," she said.

Dory reached out and pulled Irina to her feet. "Hold on to me," she said. "It's only 10 yards or so." As they started forward, more smoke went up into the air. The train's engine got louder.

The 10 yards seemed like 10 miles. Finally they got close enough to wave to the conductor. He gave them a sign to show them he would hold the train. But then Dory saw two men running a long way down the track.

"It's the KGB," she said in a low voice to Irina. "Let's hope the conductor doesn't wait for them too."

The conductor, however, had his eyes on only Irina and Dory. When they got up to the train, he reached down and helped Irina. When they were up the steps and inside, he closed the door behind them. The train pulled out of the station. The two Russians were left behind, running along the track.

Irina fell into a seat. Dory dropped down beside her. Irina asked, "Are we safe?"

"I think so," said a man behind them. The man looked out over the top of Irina's chair.

"Steve," Dory said. "You made it! How did you get here? What happened?"

"It was close," Steve laughed. "The baron was pretty mad. But there was nothing he could do. He must have thought that those guys in the helicopter would see you. So I just grabbed my skis and took off. I followed your trail down. When I saw you reach town, I started to look for a telephone. Then I saw you head down the wrong street, but I knew you'd find the right one. I needed to get to a telephone right away."

"You should have helped us," said Dory.

"I did help. I made an important telephone call."

Irina smiled. "American Embassy in Geneva?"

Steve shook his head. "No time. It would have taken too long to get through. I called Barbara Cole in Mürren. I told her the story and asked *her* to call the American Embassy.

They will have someone at the station when we reach Geneva. You can be sure of that. And I know the Russians will stay away. They won't want trouble that will make them look bad. They will have to let you defect."

Irina sat back in her seat. Then she smiled again, a bigger smile this time. She looked at Dory. "Next year," she said. "Next year we race in Europe—on same side."

Dory smiled back. She hadn't really thought about that. She found herself staring at Irina. That fall in the last race. Had Irina planned it? Or had it just happened?

Then Dory looked away. She looked out the window at the beautiful, high mountains and the bright, clear sky. She would just have to wait until next year to find out.